God Bless Me,
God Bless You

To ....

From ....

Published by Baker Books
a division of Baker Book House Company
P.O. Box 6287, Grand Rapids, MI 49516-6287

ISBN 0-8010-4488-X

Printed and bound in Singapore

For current information about all releases from Baker Book House, visit our web site:
http://www.bakerbooks.com

God Bless Me, God Bless You

Words by Lois Rock
Pictures by John Bendall-Brunello

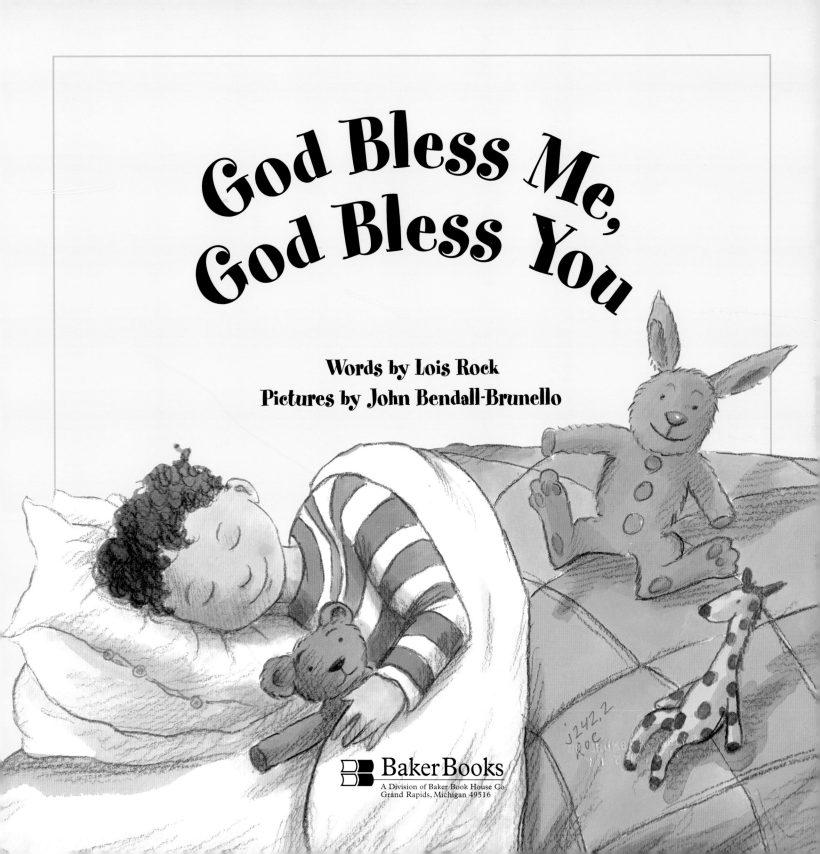

Baker Books

A Division of Baker Book House Co
Grand Rapids, Michigan 49516

The day is over, night is near,
There's one more thing to do –
Let's say a prayer to God above:
God bless me, God bless you.

Dear God, bless everything you made,
The daytime and the night,

The sun, the moon and all the stars
That shine with twinkling light.

God bless the hills that stand so tall,
God bless the fields so green,
God bless the seas, God bless the waves,
God bless each rippling stream.

Let flowers close their petals now
And may the night-time breeze
Blow gently through the grasses and
The whispering forest trees.

Remember, too, O Maker God,
The creatures of the day.
In cosy homes may each one sleep
The night-time hours away.

Now all the creatures of the night
Awake, and softly creep

On grey and silver woodland paths
While we are fast asleep.

Please take good care of those we love
Who help us every day,
Who bring us all the things we need
And still have time to play.

Take care of loved ones far away,
Who watch the shining moon
And think of us with sighs and smiles
And hope to see us soon.

Now, as the earth turns, other lands
Can see the sun above.
May all the peoples of the world
Find happiness and love.

Dear God, now let me say goodbye
To all that I have done.
Help me forgive the horrid things,
Remember all the fun.

May I sleep deep and dreamily
Till darkness slips away.
I'll wake up with the golden sun
All ready for the day.

Now night has come and we are tired.
There's nothing left to do,
For God is love, and God above
Will bless both me and you.